HILARION

HILARION

Daniel Curley

Illustrated by Judith Gwyn Brown

Houghton Mifflin Company Boston 1979

For all my girls

Library of Congress Cataloging in Publication Data

Curley, Daniel.
  Hilarion.

  SUMMARY: At the turn of the century Hilarion joins four
other men from Linsk and finds the streets of America paved
with gold.
  [1. Emigration and immigration – Fiction. 2. New
York (City) – Fiction] I. Brown, Judith Gwyn.
II. Title.
PZ7.C929Hi   [Fic]   79-11749

ISBN 0-395-28268-3

CONTENTS

1.

The Hard Times of the Men of Linsk

The four men of Linsk were in a sad way. They were cold and hungry and discouraged. They had come to America to make their fortunes, but their luck was bad. They had meant to send money back home to pay for steamship tickets for their wives and children. Instead, their wives had been sending them packages of food — a cheese, some dried herring, hard, hard bread. But now it had been a long time since such a package had reached them. So they were having a meeting to decide what to do.

"We'll have to give up and go back to Linsk," said Stefan the tailor. It was a good thing for the men of Linsk that he was with them, for without him they would have been much more cold and ragged than they were.

"How can we let everyone know we have failed?" said Mikhail the carpenter. The men of Linsk were indeed lucky to have him with them, for without him the wind would have blown in more fiercely around windows and doors, and they would have been even more cold and wretched than they were.

"How can we go on any longer without our wives and children?" said Konrad the shoemaker. The men of Linsk thanked their stars that he was with them, for without him their feet would have been much more cold and sore than they were.

"We have no money for food," said Tomasz the butcher. "We have no money for fuel. So we certainly have no money for steamship tickets." The men of Linsk were not particularly lucky to have Tomasz with them. In his sleep he talked of steaks and chops and sausages, and made them all even more hungry and miserable than before.

The men of Linsk sat and looked at each other. They sat on the floor, of course, for they had long since burned up all the chairs. They sat wrapped in their thin coats, huddled against the cold. Stefan the tailor watched them carefully to see that they didn't strain the seams of their coats, for he knew he would not be able to mend them again, the cloth was so worn and threadbare.

"Look out, Tomasz," Stefan would say, "you're sitting on your coattails. Ease off, there." Or he would say, "Don't stretch your arms like that, Konrad, or you'll ruin everything."

The only other sound was the tap, tap of Mikhail's caulking mallet as he drove more rags into a crack under the windowsill.

"We could be deported," Konrad said.

"Deported?" Stefan said.

"What's deported?" Tomasz said.

"I heard people talking about it," Konrad said. "It means sent home."

"Who'd send us home?" Mikhail said over his shoulder. Tap, tap.

"The police," Konrad said.

"Perhaps you'd better explain yourself, Konrad," Stefan said. The others thought Konrad wasn't very bright, but he was their friend — and a good shoemaker — and from their very own Linsk — and they were always patient with him.

"I was in the coffee house," Konrad said.

"What were you doing in the coffee house?" Mikhail said sternly. Bang. Bang.

"Smelling the coffee," Konrad said. "It's free. They let me smell all I want."

"Oh, very well," Mikhail said. He couldn't see that smelling coffee was in any way dishonorable to the good name of Linsk. "Just so long as you don't look as if you want any," he said. Tap, tap.

"I hope I know better than that," Konrad said.

He looked hurt, so Stefan said. "Of course you do, Konrad. We all know that. But what is deported? How does it work?"

"There was a very bad man," Konrad said. "He had done — I don't know what he had done — but it was

3

very, very bad. So the police made him go back to his village where he had learned to do such things and where no one will mind so much."

"I don't see how that helps us," Tomasz said.

"The police bought him a steamship ticket and made him go. I heard all about it in the coffee house. It was our very own policeman who stands on our corner who caught him and made him go. Mr. Murphy is his name —"

"The bad man?" Stefan said.

"No," Konrad said. "Mr. Murphy is the policeman."

"Do you think Mr. Murphy would send us home if we did something bad?" Mikhail said.

"But what could we do bad?" Tomasz said.

"We could rob a bank," Mikhail said.

"Oh, no," the others said.

"We could kidnap the mayor," Stefan said.

"Oh, no," the others said.

"We could hold up a streetcar and make the conductor take us wherever we wanted to go," Tomasz said.

"To Linsk," all the others shouted and laughed a half-laugh, Ha. "Oh, no," they said.

The men of Linsk hugged their knees under their coats but were careful not to strain the seams. Sometimes they blew on their fingers. Sometimes they sighed. Tap, tap went Mikhail's caulking mallet.

Just as they were looking at each other for the hundredth time and sighing little frosty sighs, white puffs in

5

the cold air, they heard someone coming up the stairs. They listened, divided between hope and fear.

"Suppose it's good news," Konrad said.

"Suppose it's the landlord for the rent," Tomasz said.

The steps hesitated on the floor below, stopped at Mrs. Altieri's door, and started up the last flight of stairs.

"Suppose it's a job," Mikhail said.

"Suppose it's a bill," Stefan said.

They were all silent after that. The steps came on up the stairs and along the hall. The men of Linsk held their breath, not a single smoke signal among them. And then the steps stopped in front of their very own door.

Then there was a knock. It was a very gentle, very polite knock.

"It can't be the landlord," Tomasz whispered.

"It can't be a bill," Stefan whispered.

There was another knock, even more gentle than the first.

"It can't be a job," Mikhail whispered.

"It might be good news," Konrad said right out loud, and he opened the door.

At first all they saw was a waistcoat. It was an enormous waistcoat and filled the doorway from side to side. It was brightly embroidered with flowers and birds. Bursts of sun. And gleams of stars.

"Linsk," said all the men of Linsk together.

There was no doubt that it was the work of Linsk, the careful, loving work of a woman of Linsk.

Of course there had to be a man inside the waistcoat — and there was — but the men of Linsk were so astonished — and pleased — and dismayed — that for a moment they didn't think of that. Then the man lowered a large trunk from his shoulder and grasped it in his arms to maneuver it through the door.

Now, of course, the waistcoat was hidden but the trunk was no less wonderful. It was crossed with straps and bound with buckles. Batten strips ran across it from side to side and painted all along it was one mysterious word: HILARION.

2.

Hilarion

The trunk stood in the middle of the floor, and the men of Linsk continued to stare at the wonderful word. The huge man stood behind the trunk, and the men of Linsk slowly raised their eyes again to the wonderful waistcoat. At last they looked above the waistcoat to the face.

And such a face. It was full and large as was right for a man so tall and broad. But it was scarcely the face of a man — unless of a very young man. It was more the face of a child. A smiling child. A child with quiet and watchful eyes.

Then the great mouth opened, and the men of Linsk quickly put their hands over their ears, because they were afraid that the voice would be as big as the mouth and they would be deafened. But in truth the voice was soft and gentle — but merry, too, a real child's voice. The men of Linsk as quickly took their hands down from their ears.

"Would you repeat that, please?" Stefan said. The others all nodded.

"My name is Hilarion," Hilarion said.

Suddenly he hopped over the trunk, flung open his arms, and rushed toward them. "I've found you," he shouted.

Now the men of Linsk were really deafened. They didn't hear what he said, and they were frightened by his noise and violence. They sprang into the corners of the room and kept one eye on him and one on the door.

Hilarion stood in the middle of the room. The men of Linsk froze against the walls.

"Your name is Hilarion," Mikhail said. He was very brave, but that was all he could think of to say.

Hilarion nodded and laughed a laugh that made them all feel very much better. They thought of their own children back in Linsk and were cheered.

"You seem to be a friendly fellow," Konrad said. "Give us your hand."

Hilarion laughed again and put out his hand to Konrad. His hand grip seemed to reach halfway up to Konrad's elbow, but Konrad said later that it felt — he didn't know really — it felt the way a baby must feel when its mother holds it — the strongest and yet the gentlest thing in the world.

"My name is Konrad," Konrad said. "I — "

"I know you, Konrad," Hilarion said. "I come from Linsk. My mother has sent me out to seek my fortune, and the wives of the men of Linsk have sent me out to find their husbands."

"What men of Linsk might these be?" Stefan said.

"Why," Hilarion said, "you, for one, Stefan the tailor."

"You are from Linsk, you say?" Stefan said.

"Oh, yes," Hilarion said. "Of course I am from Linsk. How else would I know you?"

"If you are from Linsk," Stefan said, "how is it that we don't know you?"

"You are rather large to be overlooked, you know," Mikhail said.

"But I was little when you left," Hilarion said.

"Who is your father?" Mikhail said.

"Where do you live?" Tomasz said.

"What's the name of the mayor?" Konrad said.

"Where did you get that real Linsk waistcoat?" Stefan said.

Hilarion looked from one to another in amazement. He had found the men of Linsk after many difficulties, and he thought his troubles were now over. He had expected a joyous meeting with delight and warmth on all sides, but he found only suspicion and coldness.

There were reasons, however, for the hesitation of the men of Linsk. For one thing, they couldn't tell who Hilarion really was. To be sure, he was frank and merry, but they were afraid he might be the frank and merry agent of the landlord come to throw them out of the cold, drafty room into the colder, draftier street. And even if Hilarion was who he claimed to be, there was still a difficulty. The men of Linsk were, quite simply, ashamed to be seen by anyone from Linsk, poor as they were, cold, hungry, and completely unsuccessful in finding their fortune in America where, as anyone knows, gold is to be picked up in the streets.

Hilarion now seemed to be about to break into tears. His mouth opened as if for a bellow, but all he said was, "Oh, my." He crept over to the wall and sat with his knees under his chin like all the rest of them.

Now, the men of Linsk were truly sorry to see Hilarion like this. A light seemed to have gone out of their own lives as his face darkened. But they were still reluctant to believe who he was and admit their failure.

Hilarion looked up. He had thought of something. "As to your questions," he said, "my mother embroidered my waistcoat. Wladyslaw Brzesc is always the mayor. I live at the corner of the High Street and Zygmundt Lane. And I have no father."

"Wrong," Mikhail, Tomasz, and Stefan shouted. "No one lives on the corner of the High Street and Zygmundt Lane."

"The Tailors' Guildhall is on that corner," Stefan said.

"The Covered Market is on that corner," Tomasz said.

"The Lumberyard is on that corner," Mikhail said.

"But," Konrad said, "there is a fourth corner, and I think — I seem to remember — a little shop."

"Of course," Stefan said. "I remember now. I bought a pair of shoelaces there once."

"Stefan — " Konrad said reproachfully.

"Your shop was closed that day," Stefan said. "It really was. I rang and pounded, and you were nowhere to be found."

"That's right," Tomasz said. "The woman in the shop — "

"My mother," Hilarion said.

"The woman in the shop mended the sleeve of my coat one day," Tomasz said.

"How did that happen?" Stefan said.

"That was a day when you were off making a suit at somebody's farm. Some Stanislaw or Casimir something."

"Casimir Gniezno," Stefan said. "That's all right."

"Well," Tomasz said, "you certainly do seem to be from Linsk."

"And there is no doubt we all are from Linsk," Konrad said.

Hilarion smiled and the room seemed brighter and even a little warmer.

"But — " Mikhail said. The light went out and the temperature dropped twenty-two degrees.

"But," Mikhail went on, "now that it is clear that you are really from Linsk, what can we do for you?"

This was not at all what Hilarion expected. For a moment he was silent. "Why," he said, "I thought I might do something for you — I have gifts — in my trunk — warm clothing — food — other things — "

"Really?" Konrad said. He was excited and even took a step toward the trunk.

"Konrad, you ninny," the men of Linsk said. "Sometimes you act as if you came from Minsk."

"I mean," Mikhail said, "here we are, successful businessmen from Linsk. What do we need with gifts? After all, it isn't as if we couldn't make our way in America. It isn't as if we came from Pinsk."

"Where did you get these things?" Konrad said sadly. He took a step backward away from the trunk and tried very hard not to look cold or hungry or homesick.

"Why, from your wives, of course," Hilarion said. "When word got out in the city that I was coming to America to seek my fortune, your wives brought me these things to bring to you."

"Foolish women," Tomasz said. "They must think they are married to men from some such wretched place as Zinsk."

"Or Finsk," Stefan said.

"Then I've carried all this all this way for nothing," Hilarion said.

"No, no," Stefan said. "Not for nothing, Hilarion. Not so at all. We are very grateful to you."

"Oh, yes," Konrad said.

"When we find time," Mikhail said, "we will take these things to our houses and be glad to have them."

"But don't you live here?" Hilarion said.

"Here?" Mikhail said. He laughed scornfully.

14

"Of course not," Tomasz said.

"This is just our office," Stefan said. "We are from Linsk, remember, and are now American businessmen, and this is our meeting to share our profits. After all, it isn't as if we came from Finsk."

"Or Pinsk," Mikhail said.

"Or Zinsk," Tomasz said.

"Or Minsk," Konrad said finally after the others all stared at him. He knew the others must be right, for they were so much smarter than he was. But he thought it was very hard indeed to pretend not to be cold and hungry while he was standing there looking at a trunk full of good things to eat and his own warm clothes. It was much harder than smelling coffee at the coffee house.

"Sometimes we can't get home for weeks on end," Tomasz said.

"I can see I've got a lot to learn," Hilarion said.

"Don't worry, Hilarion," Stefan said. "We'll all help you."

Hilarion stood up and beat his arms about him so that the others had to be very spry to keep from getting their ears boxed or their heads knocked quite off. "You American businessmen certainly keep your offices cold enough," he said. He blew an experimental breath to show how cold the room was, and they all disappeared in the great cloud that filled the room.

"The cold keeps our heads clear for business," Mikhail

said, panting. It was very hard work dodging Hilarion's flailing arms in the fog, and they were all getting out of breath.

"Well," Hilarion said, "you must be very successful businessmen indeed, and everything I have ever heard about America must be true if you just leave your money lying around for me to pick off the tops of doors."

Since Hilarion was standing up, his head was above the level of the fog he had made by careless breathing, and he saw on the top of the door frame a very dusty coin. He picked up the coin and rubbed it on his pants — he looked hastily around for his mother before he remembered she was back in Linsk and couldn't scold him for getting his pants dirty. When he looked at the coin again, he saw that it was bright gold. There was no telling how many years it had lain there.

"I've always heard," Hilarion said, "that America is where you get ahead by picking up gold just lying around, so I'll start getting ahead with this, and, who knows, soon I may be as successful as any of you. But the first step in getting ahead is getting something good to eat. I don't suppose you could stop business long enough to join me?"

"Oh, no," Stefan said. "Business first."

"I must remember that," Hilarion said. "Business first."

The men of Linsk looked very green indeed as Hilarion put the tiny coin in his very large pocket.

"Perhaps things would go easier," Hilarion said, "if I just moved my valise out of the way."

"Valise?" Konrad said.

Hilarion obviously referred to his trunk, which was so big and heavy that two of the men of Linsk could scarcely have moved it. But Hilarion picked it up and put it against the wall as easily as if it had been a lunch pail. He smiled at all of them, patted his pocket, and was gone.

The men of Linsk were glum enough when he had left. They had their pride all right, but they also had empty stomachs. They stared at each other in something very like despair, and then they all sprang up and frantically searched above the doors and above the windows but found nothing.

When Hilarion returned, they were back against the walls with their knees up and their heads down. They were so discouraged that they forgot to be careful of their seams and their coattails, and Stefan was too hungry to scold them about it.

3.

The Feast

Hilarion brought back with him a huge meat pie and a pot of tea nearly big enough for the Boston Tea Party. He spread the good things on his trunk and began to eat. "Are you sure you wouldn't like to join me?" he said. "There's more than enough for everyone."

"That's very kind of you," Konrad said. "I'd love to." He got his cup and cleared the spider web out of it and dusted his plate and began to eat.

The others looked very disapproving. But when Hilarion asked them again, Stefan said, "We finished our business while you were gone, so a little snack wouldn't be a bad idea at all. There's nothing like a good stroke of work to make you want a bite of something or other."

"Just to be sociable," Tomasz said.

"You're very kind, I'm sure," Mikhail said.

And they all got their cups and emptied out the pencil stubs and buttons and nails and tacks and needles, a little of this and a little of that, a bit of everything and nothing very much.

"Now," Hilarion said, "if it were just a trifle warmer in here, we'd be as snug as anyone could wish."

"Now that business is over," Stefan said, "it does seem a bit brisk in here, since you happen to mention it."

"Then if you don't mind," Hilarion said, "we'll just have a little fire. Will you please hold your plates and your cups for a moment while I open my grip?"

The men of Linsk took their plates and cups off the trunk and stood back against the wall. It was just like a stand-up birthday party, because they found their hands full of good things but there was no way to eat them. Their mouths opened and closed hungrily as the delicious smell of the meat pie rose before them, and they nearly cried with hunger and impatience.

Meanwhile, Hilarion unbuckled and unstrapped and unlocked and opened his trunk. Bang went the lid back against the wall. Tomasz had to jump quickly aside to avoid being mashed like a fly.

"Sausage," he muttered as he licked a little spilled tea off the back of his hand.

Hilarion had the trunk open barely a minute, but a wonderful mixture of smells escaped into the room. Cheese. And dried herring. And sour-rye bread. Pickles. Beet soup. Coffee. Spices.

"It smells like home," Konrad said.

"They can't match that smell in Minskpinskzinskfinsk," the men of Linsk said.

"I don't know about Minskpinskzinskfinsk," Hilarion

said, "but it certainly does smell like Linsk." And he slammed the lid and locked and strapped and buckled and shut it all up.

But he had taken out of the trunk a great bundle of firewood. "My mother says," he said, "that in New York there are no trees and that I must have my own wood for the first year until I discover what everyone does where there is no forest to cut in."

"That's a very wise mother," Mikhail said. The smell of the wood of Linsk was for him as great a treat as the smell of food. He put his plate and cup on the floor and picked up one piece of the wood. He held it in his hands and turned it and studied the grain and thought of all the things he could make of it. But he settled on a doll for his youngest child.

He no sooner thought of the doll than he picked up his knife and began to carve. Curls and slivers of wood began to fall about his feet, and Hilarion said, "Just what we need to start the fire."

Hilarion all the while was busily laying the fire in the old iron stove that had stood against the wall, rusty and discouraged, for months now. It was so long since the stove had had anything to do with fire that the men of Linsk were convinced that out of resentment it spent all its time radiating cold rather than heat.

But now as Hilarion put in the paper that had covered the pie and the shavings that had covered Mikhail's feet and some kindling, which he split with his thumbnail, and some solid chunks, the stove relented and became a stove again rather than an iceberg. Even before the fire was lighted, they all felt warmer.

"And now, gentlemen," Hilarion said, "shall we eat?"

They put their cups down on the trunk. Up to now the cups had mainly warmed their hands. And they began to eat. A good part of the pleasure for the men of Linsk was in knowing that however much they ate there would be some left over for tomorrow and the next day and the day after that. They sighed contentedly. Life was suddenly a hopeful thing once more.

But then they thought of Hilarion's size and began secretly to watch him eat. They soon learned, however, that he ate very little more than they did, and they sighed once more. They even laughed when they saw that their sighs didn't hang in the air like clouds now that the room was warm.

Finally they had eaten as much as they could hold, and they were warm and content by the fire.

"But, Hilarion," Konrad said, "where did you get that shawl?"

All the men of Linsk now noticed for the first time that Hilarion was wearing a richly woven shawl from the old country.

"Is it from Linsk?" Stefan asked, although they all knew perfectly well that it wasn't a Linsk pattern.

"Oh, no," Hilarion said, and he looked grave and pleased.

And the others all hastily shook their heads and said it wasn't from Minsk or Pinsk or Zinsk or Finsk. And they wondered all the more, since they knew very well that when Hilarion went out for the pie he was in his shirt-sleeves in spite of the bitter cold.

"Here," Stefan said, "there's a rip in it. Let me just mend it for you."

Hilarion at once took the shawl from his shoulders and passed it to Stefan. Stefan trembled with pleasure as he ran the cloth through his hands. He felt rich. He had almost forgotten the feel of such material. He mended it lovingly, and when he was done, even the most careful eye couldn't find where the rip was.

"But where did it come from?" Konrad said again.

"Well — " Hilarion said.

The men of Linsk all knew there was going to be a story, so they lay down around the stove to listen comfortably.

4.

The Shawl

Hilarion told them that when he went out to get the pie and the tea, he stepped into an ordinary, everyday sort of street. It was jammed from house front to house front with people and horses and wagons and indescribable things. Laundry hung high above the street on lines stretched between the buildings and flapped and snapped like flags at a parade. Suits on racks in front of shops danced in the winter wind. Fruit, vegetables, meat, fish, bread were all displayed in shop windows and then repeated on the line of handcarts along each curb.

And the handcarts had more. They had old clothes, old books, old pictures, jumbled heaps of shoes, rusty hardware — junk no one knew the name of but everyone stopped to look at and some even bought, not knowing quite what to do with it but seeing at a glance that it was so obviously useful they had to have it. And at the price, who could pass it up?

In the middle of the street, there was a line of fine horses and great wagons, and thin horses and wagons so

reet that Hilarion went about his business without pay-
g much attention except to keep from bumping into
ple or stepping on babies or cats. When he had first
me along that way, looking for the house of the men of
nsk, he had noticed a shop where he could get a fine
, so now he went on steadily toward it.
But at the corner of the block, he was forced to stop
a moment. It couldn't be said that a crowd had
ected, because there was a crowd everywhere. But
arion noticed that no one was talking and that they
e all facing something in the middle of the street.
hen he looked over the massed heads before him, he
saw a brewer's wagon that was tipping danger-
y. The load of kegs seemed about to topple into the
t. "A broken wheel," Hilarion said to himself. The
s were plunging and slipping as they strained
st the load. Their hooves rang on the stones and
ered sparks all about.
oliceman was trying to control the horses and the
e all at once, but he was not having much luck with
rses. It was, in fact, that very Mr. Murphy whom
n of Linsk had known for so long, but whose name
d had just learned in the coffee house.
nd back, stand back," Mr. Murphy shouted.
crowd stood well back. They wanted no part of
tic horses or the toppling kegs of beer.
ebody grab the horses," Mr. Murphy shouted.
one stepped forward. "They're making it

rickety they seemed to be afraid to move, and squeaked
and grumbled whenever the line inched forward a step.
There were the shiny bright wagons of the brewers with
their huge and shining horses. The feathered feet of the
horses clattered on the cobblestones. And the slow and
heavy coal carts driven by men so covered with coal dust
that their eyes shone out like moons. Towering loads of
hay for the livery stables. Heavy wagons of the timber
merchants, creaking under loads of great balks and massive tree trunks just unloaded from ships at the harbor.
Loads of sacks of flour. Bakers' carts that smelled so
good that people looked around hungrily for something
to eat and bought the first thing that came to hand, hot
chestnuts or pickled eels, periwinkles or smoking sausage. And wagons full of who knows what, but something that somebody sold and somebody bought and that
helped everybody to get along somehow.

Everywhere there wasn't something else, there were
people, moving slowly like fish against a current, stopping in groups or by twos, and all talking at once, even
those by themselves. "Come buy, come buy," the merchants shouted from the doors of their shops. "Come
buy, come buy," the hucksters shouted from beside their
barrows. "Come buy, come buy," the peddlers shouted
as they held up some item from their packs. "Any
rags? Any bottles?" the junkmen shouted from their
rickety wagons.

In short, it was such an ordinary, everyday sort of

st
in
pe
co
Li
pie
for
col
Hil
wer
W
first
ousl
stree
horse
again
show
A
peopl
the ho
the me
Konra
"Sta
The
the fra
"Son
But no

worse," Mr. Murphy shouted. "Quick. Help. Somebody go to the timber yard for a crane. They'll kill her."

Mr. Murphy tried to catch one of the horses by the
reins but was knocked back against the crowd. The people lowered him gently to the ground. "Get a doctor,"
someone said.

Near where Mr. Murphy lay in the street, two men
were holding a woman who was crying and struggling
and trying to run toward the wagon. Hilarion didn't
know what was going on, but he did know that the
horses would hurt themselves or somebody else if they
went on this way. He forced his way quickly through
the crowd. "Excuse me," he said. "Sorry," he said.

Of course most of the people there didn't understand
a word he said, for they spoke twenty different languages
in that street, but they saw what he was about and they
let him pass. He stepped to the horses' heads and made
two quick passes with his hands, like a boy catching
flies. He had each horse by its bridle, and they were
soon quiet.

"Unhitch the horses," Hilarion said. The teamster
didn't understand what he said, but he knew what had
to be done, so he jumped down from the wagon and
unhitched the horses and led them away.

Hilarion didn't expect any great praise or reward for
calming the horses, but he was surprised to see that
everyone was still staring at the wagon and that the
woman was still crying and struggling.

"What's wrong?" Hilarion said. People were shouting at him and pointing to the wagon, but Hilarion couldn't understand a word. He was thoroughly confused.

He looked at the wagon and saw that a wheel had sunk into soft dirt where workmen had dug up the street. Even as he looked, the wheel sank a little deeper. The wagon lurched, the kegs rumbled, and the woman screamed. The bed of the wagon was now almost down to the ground.

But when the woman screamed, Hilarion took heart. He had heard her scream, "My child," in a language that could be understood any day in Linsk — or Minsk or Pinsk or Zinsk or Finsk.

Hilarion went to her. "What's wrong?" he said.

She was calmed by being spoken to in her own language and said, "My child is under the wagon. Please help me."

So Hilarion lay down beside the wagon and looked under while the beer kegs joggled and jarred above him and threatened every minute to become an avalanche. Sure enough, there was the child, a little girl with her dress caught on a little hook on a bit of chain. She was quite unhurt, although she was stretched out flat and the wagon was close above her. She had a red ball in her hand, and Hilarion knew at once that she had chased it under the wagon and been caught there.

Hilarion peeked at her through the spokes of the wheel. "Boo," he said.

"Boo," the girl said and giggled.

So Hilarion stood up and took hold of the wagon and lifted the wheel out of the hole and eased it forward onto solid ground.

The mother ran forward and freed the child from the hook. Hilarion leaned against the wagon and caught his breath. The crowd cheered and turned to other things, except for one man who came forward and said, "You're a fine strong young man, and I wish I were a blacksmith so I could give you a job."

"Well, I'm not a blacksmith either," Hilarion said, "although to be sure I'll need a job."

The man looked shrewdly at Hilarion. "Nor am I a brewer," he said, "to be needing strong teamsters."

"No more am I a teamster," Hilarion said.

"You have a way with horses," the man said.

"But I haven't the skill to drive a great team through these streets," Hilarion said.

"Nor am I the kind of merchant to need men to lift great bales in my warehouses," the man said.

"More's the pity," Hilarion said, "because I think I could lift bales if they came in my way."

"I think you could," the man said, and he glanced at the wagon, where the teamster was just hitching the horses up again. "But tell me, young man," he said, "what exactly do you do?"

"I am a watchmaker," Hilarion said proudly. "I am just out of my apprenticeship and ready to go to work."

rickety they seemed to be afraid to move, and squeaked and grumbled whenever the line inched forward a step. There were the shiny bright wagons of the brewers with their huge and shining horses. The feathered feet of the horses clattered on the cobblestones. And the slow and heavy coal carts driven by men so covered with coal dust that their eyes shone out like moons. Towering loads of hay for the livery stables. Heavy wagons of the timber merchants, creaking under loads of great balks and massive tree trunks just unloaded from ships at the harbor. Loads of sacks of flour. Bakers' carts that smelled so good that people looked around hungrily for something to eat and bought the first thing that came to hand, hot chestnuts or pickled eels, periwinkles or smoking sausage. And wagons full of who knows what, but something that somebody sold and somebody bought and that helped everybody to get along somehow.

Everywhere there wasn't something else, there were people, moving slowly like fish against a current, stopping in groups or by twos, and all talking at once, even those by themselves. "Come buy, come buy," the merchants shouted from the doors of their shops. "Come buy, come buy," the hucksters shouted from beside their barrows. "Come buy, come buy," the peddlers shouted as they held up some item from their packs. "Any rags? Any bottles?" the junkmen shouted from their rickety wagons.

In short, it was such an ordinary, everyday sort of

street that Hilarion went about his business without paying much attention except to keep from bumping into people or stepping on babies or cats. When he had first come along that way, looking for the house of the men of Linsk, he had noticed a shop where he could get a fine pie, so now he went on steadily toward it.

But at the corner of the block, he was forced to stop for a moment. It couldn't be said that a crowd had collected, because there was a crowd everywhere. But Hilarion noticed that no one was talking and that they were all facing something in the middle of the street.

When he looked over the massed heads before him, he first saw a brewer's wagon that was tipping dangerously. The load of kegs seemed about to topple into the street. "A broken wheel," Hilarion said to himself. The horses were plunging and slipping as they strained against the load. Their hooves rang on the stones and showered sparks all about.

A policeman was trying to control the horses and the people all at once, but he was not having much luck with the horses. It was, in fact, that very Mr. Murphy whom the men of Linsk had known for so long, but whose name Konrad had just learned in the coffee house.

"Stand back, stand back," Mr. Murphy shouted.

The crowd stood well back. They wanted no part of the frantic horses or the toppling kegs of beer.

"Somebody grab the horses," Mr. Murphy shouted. But no one stepped forward. "They're making it

28

worse," Mr. Murphy shouted. "Quick. Help. Somebody go to the timber yard for a crane. They'll kill her."

Mr. Murphy tried to catch one of the horses by the reins but was knocked back against the crowd. The people lowered him gently to the ground. "Get a doctor," someone said.

Near where Mr. Murphy lay in the street, two men were holding a woman who was crying and struggling and trying to run toward the wagon. Hilarion didn't know what was going on, but he did know that the horses would hurt themselves or somebody else if they went on this way. He forced his way quickly through the crowd. "Excuse me," he said. "Sorry," he said.

Of course most of the people there didn't understand a word he said, for they spoke twenty different languages in that street, but they saw what he was about and they let him pass. He stepped to the horses' heads and made two quick passes with his hands, like a boy catching flies. He had each horse by its bridle, and they were soon quiet.

"Unhitch the horses," Hilarion said. The teamster didn't understand what he said, but he knew what had to be done, so he jumped down from the wagon and unhitched the horses and led them away.

Hilarion didn't expect any great praise or reward for calming the horses, but he was surprised to see that everyone was still staring at the wagon and that the woman was still crying and struggling.

"What's wrong?" Hilarion said. People were shouting at him and pointing to the wagon, but Hilarion couldn't understand a word. He was thoroughly confused.

He looked at the wagon and saw that a wheel had sunk into soft dirt where workmen had dug up the street. Even as he looked, the wheel sank a little deeper. The wagon lurched, the kegs rumbled, and the woman screamed. The bed of the wagon was now almost down to the ground.

But when the woman screamed, Hilarion took heart. He had heard her scream, "My child," in a language that could be understood any day in Linsk — or Minsk or Pinsk or Zinsk or Finsk.

Hilarion went to her. "What's wrong?" he said.

She was calmed by being spoken to in her own language and said, "My child is under the wagon. Please help me."

So Hilarion lay down beside the wagon and looked under while the beer kegs joggled and jarred above him and threatened every minute to become an avalanche. Sure enough, there was the child, a little girl with her dress caught on a little hook on a bit of chain. She was quite unhurt, although she was stretched out flat and the wagon was close above her. She had a red ball in her hand, and Hilarion knew at once that she had chased it under the wagon and been caught there.

Hilarion peeked at her through the spokes of the wheel. "Boo," he said.

"Boo," the girl said and giggled.

So Hilarion stood up and took hold of the wagon and lifted the wheel out of the hole and eased it forward onto solid ground.

The mother ran forward and freed the child from the hook. Hilarion leaned against the wagon and caught his breath. The crowd cheered and turned to other things, except for one man who came forward and said, "You're a fine strong young man, and I wish I were a blacksmith so I could give you a job."

"Well, I'm not a blacksmith either," Hilarion said, "although to be sure I'll need a job."

The man looked shrewdly at Hilarion. "Nor am I a brewer," he said, "to be needing strong teamsters."

"No more am I a teamster," Hilarion said.

"You have a way with horses," the man said.

"But I haven't the skill to drive a great team through these streets," Hilarion said.

"Nor am I the kind of merchant to need men to lift great bales in my warehouses," the man said.

"More's the pity," Hilarion said, "because I think I could lift bales if they came in my way."

"I think you could," the man said, and he glanced at the wagon, where the teamster was just hitching the horses up again. "But tell me, young man," he said, "what exactly do you do?"

"I am a watchmaker," Hilarion said proudly. "I am just out of my apprenticeship and ready to go to work."

Here he stopped and stared at the man, who was laughing and crying and holding his sides.

"You?" the man said. "A watchmaker? You?"

"I," Hilarion said. "A watchmaker. I."

"I'm sorry," the man said. "I didn't mean to laugh, but it was so unexpected. I mean, there you were, catching horses like flies and lifting wagons like satchels, and now you tell me you are a watchmaker. I mean, all those tiny, tiny springs and little delicate wheels."

"I am a watchmaker," Hilarion said.

"With your great hands and thick fingers — "

"I am a watchmaker. I have letters from my old master, Master Tadeusz of Linsk," Hilarion said.

"Master Tadeusz," the man said. "Of Linsk. That's a different matter entirely. I happen to be a watchmaker myself, and I could use a good young man. Come and see me at my shop." He wanted to be sure he had Hilarion's name right, so he made him spell it out.

Mr. Murphy, the policeman, was by now sitting up in the street. He took out his notebook, and he licked his pencil, and he carefully drew a large star, and beside the star he wrote HILARION.

The watchmaker then gave Hilarion careful instructions how to find his shop. And he went about his business.

Hilarion was pleased to observe that not all American businessmen sat about fasting in icy rooms and wore coats severely strained as to seams and tails. He had

33

begun to think that getting ahead in America wouldn't be a very comfortable thing. He was about to go about his business — the pie, of course — when the woman with the child came to him. He was sweating from his work and was beginning to shiver with chill.

"I can never thank you enough," the woman said. "But here. Take this." And she took off her shawl and gave it to him. "It got torn when I tried to get under the wagon, but it will keep you from catching cold." Then she disappeared into the crowd before Hilarion could say, "I wouldn't dream of taking your lovely shawl."

Then he did go off for the pie.

5.

Business First

No sooner had Hilarion finished telling his story than he fell fast asleep. The others talked softly among themselves and marveled more at the shawl than at the woman and more at the woman than at Hilarion's strength and courage.

"She must be a woman from the old country," Konrad said.

"Of course," Stefan said. "Didn't Hilarion understand her when she said, 'My child'?"

"And a child from the old country," Mikhail said. "How I wish I had seen her and heard her say, 'Boo.'"

They had all been warm and comfortable, full of pie and tea and the wonder of Hilarion's story. They had all been happy, and now suddenly they were sad.

"If I had seen the child," Mikhail said, "I'd have given her this doll." He held up the doll, which had taken such rapid shape in his hands. "An old-country girl would have liked an old-country doll made of old-country wood."

"But it's for your Elzbieta," Stefan said. "You made it for her."

Mikhail laughed but it was not a happy laugh. "A little while ago," he said, "we were talking of buying steamship tickets, when the truth is that we don't even have enough money to buy a postage stamp to send the doll back home."

This was so true that not even looking at the glorious remains of the marvelous pie could cheer up the men of Linsk.

"We should be glad," Konrad said.

"I suppose so," Tomasz said. "After all there is a pie for me to carve."

"That is true," Konrad said. "But I didn't mean that."

"And I have felt and sewed the wonderful shawl of home-woven cloth," Stefan said.

"That is true, too," Konrad said. "But I didn't mean that either."

"And I have smelled and felt and shaped the wood of Linsk," Mikhail said.

"That is very true," Konrad said. "But it wasn't even that I meant."

"Then what on earth did you mean?" the men of Linsk all said together.

"Why," Konrad said, "we should be glad because Hilarion has got a job." And they all knew it was so and turned to look at Hilarion where he lay asleep beside the stove, smiling in his sleep and looking even more like a happy child than ever.

"We must be very quiet," Stefan said. He carefully spread the shawl over Hilarion, who didn't stir and who went on smiling.

"We must watch over him while he sleeps," Mikhail said. He used some of the firewood and his own coat to make a screen to keep a draft from Hilarion's head.

"We must take care of him," Tomasz said, and he covered the pie and placed it on a high shelf where it would be safe.

"He has been lucky his first day in America," Konrad said, "and he has brought luck among us." He eased off Hilarion's boots and took them into the cold hall where he nailed and sewed and polished them until they were better than the day they left the shop in Linsk.

Konrad knew the shoemakers of Linsk, and it was a pleasure to him to see their fine work. But good as the work was, Konrad couldn't help making it better — first of all, because he was a better shoemaker and, most important, because he worked with love of Hilarion in his heart.

"Let us rejoice in his good fortune," the men of Linsk said. And they did rejoice quietly as they sat in the darkening room watching Hilarion sleep. The winter wind was howling and rattling the windows, but inside there was only warmth and quiet and dusk. To be sure, the stove hummed, and the fire lapped and panted softly. Hilarion breathed deeply. But these sounds only added to the peacefulness of the room. To be sure, the fire glowed red around the cracks in the stove door and cast wavering shadows on the walls. But that only made the darkness richer. To be sure, the men of Linsk rejoiced, but their rejoicing was silent. The firelight caught their smiles and their glances at each other. But that only made them rejoice the more, and gradually they all fell asleep.

In the morning they woke up and poured fresh water over the tea leaves and had a pick at the pie. Hilarion had been up a long time and had the fire roaring and the water hot. He had washed the dishes and spread the shawl on the trunk for a tablecloth. Then he had waited and watched as they woke up.

Each man woke with the sad look he had worn for months past. Then he smiled as he remembered what had happened since Hilarion came. Then he sat up hopefully and said, "Good morning, Hilarion. Good morning, all." There seemed today to be something to get up for. Something more than a warm room. Something more than the miraculous pie. They felt that somehow their luck had changed, and they were anxious to see what the day would bring.

It brought first of all Hilarion saying, "Business first."

The men of Linsk all nodded their heads. They were full of thoughts of shops where they might ask for work and plans of how they could let merchants know what they could do. All they needed was a chance to work, and their work would speak for itself. And, of course, they were right. They forgot the days of standing in line for jobs that always went to someone else. They forgot the signs on door after door: No Help Wanted. They forgot the long miles walked to find a job someone thought he had heard of, and the job was filled. They forgot everything except the hope they felt again now that Hilarion was with them.

"Business first," the men of Linsk said. And they all set out for business.

Hilarion set out, too. But what the men of Linsk didn't know was that Hilarion's idea of business was not finding the watchmaker's shop but finding the woman who had given him the shawl.

He set out with the shawl neatly folded and Mikhail's doll safely wrapped in the folds.

6.

The Talking Box

×××××××××××××

Hilarion first went and stood on the corner where he had seen the woman and child, the corner the men of Linsk had told him was Mr. Murphy's usual corner. Crowds of people swirled about him as if he were a boulder in a stream as he waited patiently. The hole in the street had been repaired. Cobblestones had been fitted into place, and there was nothing to show there had ever been a hole except for streaks of clean sand between the stones in that very small patch.

"Good morning, Hilarion," Mr. Murphy said.

"Good morning, Mr. Murphy," Hilarion said.

Neither understood a word the other said. They even pronounced each other's name in such a way that it was completely unrecognizable. But they had no trouble understanding each other's smile.

Mr. Murphy saw the carefully folded shawl and understood very well why Hilarion was there. "Yes," he said, "you're right. She does live near here, and you have only to wait long enough and you will find her."

Of course Hilarion didn't understand what Mr. Murphy was saying, but they smiled at each other again. Then Mr. Murphy went on his way slowly, smiling here and speaking there and always keeping a sharp eye out for anyone who might need to be deported. But no one seemed to be doing anything very bad that morning except some boys who were teasing a cat and a hungry horse that was nibbling hay from the great hay wagon in front of it in the line of wagons. Mr. Murphy rescued the cat and winked at the horse and went on his way, smiling and speaking and eating an apple he bought from a pushcart.

Hilarion, meanwhile, stood on the corner and looked about him. He had no way of knowing whether the woman would ever come there again, but since he didn't know where else to look, he lingered there through most of the morning.

It was a sunny winter morning without any wind, and Hilarion was quite comfortable. He was used to much colder weather in the old country. Besides, if he were really cold, he had only to go to his trunk and take out the bearskin coat his mother had made for him. "Bless you, Hilarion," his mother said. "There's no cutting and sewing in making a bearskin coat for you. It's just a matter of skinning the bear and putting buttons on the front."

Mr. Murphy and Hilarion both felt that the scene around them was a wonderfully peaceful and law-abiding scene, but they were both quite wrong. Mr. Murphy passed back and forth throughout the morning and usually stopped to exchange a few words with Hilarion, so they were standing together when they saw two men trying to load a very heavy box into a livery-stable wagon.

"Those are no teamsters," Mr. Murphy said. "They're making hard work of it."

"Those men don't know what they're doing," Hilarion said as the men tried once more to lift the box into the wagon.

"Why don't you give them a hand, my boy?" Mr. Murphy said.

"I think I'll just give them a hand," Hilarion said. Mr. Murphy nodded. Hilarion gave Mr. Murphy the shawl and the doll to hold and stepped into the street.

"Don't touch that," one of the men shouted. He was a large man with a red beard and a completely bald head. The other man was also large, but he had a black beard and so much black hair that Hilarion thought at first that the man's mother must have made him a hat out of a bear's head.

"We don't need any help," the black-bearded man said.

But of course for all Hilarion knew they were saying, "Please be careful" and "Thank you very much." So he started to take hold of the box. The red-bearded man reached inside his coat, and the black-bearded man reached for his hip pocket. But both of them glanced at Mr. Murphy, watching from the curb, and they stood motionless while Hilarion placed the box in the wagon.

"There you are," Hilarion said and smiled to show what he meant.

"Thank you, thank you," both men said, but neither smiled.

Redbeard brought his hand out from under his coat, and it was full of copper coins, which he dumped into Hilarion's hand.

"Oh, no," Hilarion said. "I don't want it." But the men jumped into the wagon and drove off before Hilarion could make them understand that he didn't want any money for such a trifling friendly service.

When Hilarion went back to reclaim the shawl and the doll from Mr. Murphy, he looked at the coins and discovered that mixed among them was a gold coin of considerable value. He showed it to Mr. Murphy.

"It must be some mistake," Mr. Murphy said.

"Surely they never meant to give me this," Hilarion said. "I must follow them and give it back."

"Fortunately," Mr. Murphy said, "I didn't like their looks and made a note of the number of the livery wagon." He tapped the pocket that held his notebook and licked his lips as if they were his pencil.

"I'm off," Hilarion said, and he began to follow the wagon as fast as he could.

He followed the wagon through rich streets and poor streets, past tenements and mansions, over one bridge and back over another, through the park and by the river. He followed it past the biggest stores and the smallest shops, past banks and newspaper offices. He even passed the watchmaker's shop where he was supposed to go to work. Finally he followed the wagon past a line of steamships tied up at the docks and came to an area of old warehouses in a street that was quite deserted. The warehouses still smelled beautifully of spices and coffee, of rare woods and tobacco, but they all seemed abandoned now.

Hilarion caught up with the men while they were tying a rope to the box so they could hoist it through a warehouse door. "Here," Hilarion said, "look here. You've made a mistake."

"Get out of here," Redbeard said.

"If you know what's good for you," Blackbeard said.

"What's going on here?" another voice said.

Hilarion looked around, and the men looked at each other.

"I demand to know what's going on here," the voice said.

Hilarion looked at the men, and the men looked at the box.

"Answer me at once." Hilarion looked at the box. It was clearly the box that had spoken.

Hilarion laughed. This was indeed a stroke of good fortune. The box must be one of the wonderful talking boxes they have in America. Soon, no doubt, it would sing for him or play on the violin.

"Please," Hilarion said, "make it sing."

"Now we are in trouble," Blackbeard said.

"Once and for all, will you get out of here?" Redbeard said.

'Where's the little handle to make it go?" Hilarion said. He put his hand on the box to turn it around.

Both men now put their hands in their pockets, and that made Hilarion remember what he had in his own pocket. So he put his hand in his pocket, too. They all brought out their hands at once. Hilarion held the gold coin, of course. Blackbeard held a revolver. Redbeard held a nasty-looking leather club, which he smacked against the palm of his other hand with a sickening thwack.

Since no words were spoken at this point, Hilarion had no trouble understanding what the men meant. He flicked the coin with his thumb so that it caught Blackbeard on the forehead and stunned him. Then with his left hand he grabbed Redbeard by the arm and with his right hand he grabbed Blackbeard by the leg and he swung them around his head like Indian clubs. Knives and pistols and clubs and coins and bottles flew out of their pockets and rattled and clashed and clattered and smashed against the cobblestones and the warehouse wall.

Then he stacked Blackbeard and Redbeard against the wall and turned his attention to the box.

"Let me out, let me out," the box said, and something seemed to go wrong with the machinery inside, for a great banging and pounding now came out of the box.

"Perhaps it needs to be wound up again," Hilarion said. He began to look for the little handle that made it go.

Hilarion didn't find the little handle, but he did find a little hole. He put his eye to the hole to try to see what was inside, and what did he see but an eye looking right back at him. It was a very angry eye, and Hilarion started back.

"Let me out, let me out," the box shouted, and it bumped and thumped worse than ever.

"I see now," Hilarion said, for he was a bright lad and understood things very quickly. "I see now that the famous American talking box is nothing but a trick. There is a man in there all the time, and he has a violin." Then Hilarion remembered that he had also heard that the man sometimes played a piano, and he wanted to see how a piano was stored in a box that size, so he began to open the box.

When Hilarion got the box open, he saw at once that the man would have had a hard time playing a violin — which he didn't have with him anyway — or a piano, even if there had been room for it. In fact the man couldn't do much of anything except shout and glare and thump and bump, for his hands and feet were tied. A handkerchief hung around his neck and had clearly been

47

used as a gag, although he had somehow managed to free himself from it.

Hilarion could also see that this man was by no means the sort of man anyone would keep in a box in order to play the talking-box trick on people. This was clearly an important man. He wore a fine suit and a magnificent overcoat, fur-lined and with a rich fur collar. His shoes were fine and his gloves were fine. The diamond stickpin in his tie was particularly fine. And the gold watch chain on his vest could have anchored a steamer.

"Here now," Hilarion said, "just let me help you out of this." He untied the man and helped him out of the box.

"You must be voice C," the man said, "the one who came to save me. And there are the kidnappers, voices A and B." He glanced at the men still lying against the wall. He took out a rubber stamp and an ink pad from the pocket of his overcoat and stamped DEPORT on the forehead of each man.

Then the man picked the gold coin up from the street and said, "Well, my boy, you are the lucky one. This is America, you know, where you get rich just by picking up gold in the streets." And he gave the coin to Hilarion. "This is yours now."

Although Hilarion didn't know what the man was saying, he believed the coin was now his, so he put it in his pocket.

"I'll expect to see you in my office tomorrow," the man said to Hilarion and gave him a card on which was written THE MAYOR.

7.
What Else Is in the Trunk?

"You didn't go to the watchmaker's?" the men of Linsk said.

They were upset now, for they had had a very bad day. They had stood in lines, and they had walked for miles, and everywhere they had seen signs that said, No Help Wanted. In fact, the one thing that cheered them as they sat in the darkening room was the idea that Hilarion was working and really earning money. They knew somehow that he would share with them whatever he got, and they believed that sooner or later he would bring them luck. But now they learned he had spent the day in the streets looking for the woman and child, and their hopes sank.

"Now, business first," Hilarion said.

The others all remembered that that was what he had said in the morning, and they felt very sad. They didn't realize that this time he meant, Let's have another go at that pie.

But when he quickly spread the shawl on the trunk

and put out the dishes and cups and reached down the pie, Mikhail said, "Perhaps we will all feel better if we have something to eat."

"Eat something, Mikhail," Stefan said.

"Eat something, Stefan," Tomasz said.

"Eat something, Tomasz," Konrad said.

"Eat something, Konrad," Mikhail said. "We need to keep up our strength."

So they all urged each other to eat, and they all did eat. And they all did feel better.

"Now, Hilarion," Stefan said when they were done, "I hope you won't mind if I give you some advice."

"Oh, no," Hilarion said. "I want you to help me make my way in America just as you have done."

The men of Linsk were thoroughly embarrassed because Hilarion thought they were rich when they were in truth such failures. Still, they knew they must give a young man from Linsk the best advice they possibly could.

"The truth is, Hilarion," Mikhail said, "that the way to make your way is to go to the watchmaker's and set to work for him."

"I understand that," Hilarion said, "but the real truth is that the woman gave me the shawl off her back and must now be very cold."

"That is so," Konrad said.

"But if you give the shawl back to her," Tomasz said, "then you will be cold yourself."

"Oh, I have my coat in my trunk," Hilarion said, "but I can do nothing at all until I have found her and given her the shawl."

"And I want the child to have the doll," Mikhail said unexpectedly.

"And I want the woman to see that I have mended her lovely shawl as good as new," Stefan said.

"All that is as it should be," Konrad said.

"But what's to become of us, then?" Tomasz said.

"I know," Konrad said. "First thing in the morning, Hilarion can take the shawl and the doll to Mr. Murphy. After all, it is his business to stand on that corner and be on the lookout for people. If she comes there, he'll see her and give her the shawl and the doll, and Hilarion can go to the watchmaker's."

"That's a marvelous idea, Konrad," the other men of Linsk said. And Hilarion agreed that it was.

After that, they all felt relieved. No doubt the pie had something to do with it. But they felt, in any case, that tomorrow would be better. They cleaned up and washed the dishes and sat around the stove very cheerfully.

"It's going to be very cold tomorrow," Hilarion said. He went to his trunk and unbuckled and unstrapped and unlocked and opened it. He at once took out his bearskin coat and laid it aside. He did not close the trunk then but stood looking thoughtfully down into it. The men of Linsk were very curious indeed as to what Hilarion had in the trunk, but they all looked politely away while the trunk was open.

"Perhaps you want your winter coats now," Hilarion said. He held up a heavy overcoat. "This is the one Konrad's wife sent to him. 'Remind him to keep well wrapped up in the winter weather,' she said to me again and again and again."

Konrad recognized the coat at once and reached out his hand to touch it.

"These are indeed fine coats," Stefan said.

"But the truth is," Mikhail said, "they are too much in the style of Linsk. People would think we were greenhorns. It's lucky we already have good coats in the American style and can go about without being laughed at."

Hilarion looked closely at their coats, which had indeed been patched and mended until they were no particular style at all. But to be sure, except for the mayor, he had seen no one wearing a coat that was much better.

"American fashions are very strange," Hilarion said, "but I am sure you know best." Then he closed the lid of the trunk and locked and strapped and buckled it.

The men of Linsk were very sad as they thought of how cold they would be tomorrow as they walked mile after mile looking for work while the wind sifted through their worn-out coats. But they tried to be cheerful.

"After all," Stefan said, "it isn't as if we really needed the coats."

53

"It isn't as if we had gone to the gold mines in Alaska," Mikhail said, "and were shivering in the dark and snow with our pockets full of gold."

"It isn't as if we were trapping animals in the Rocky Mountains," Tomasz said, "and could find no thread to turn our rich furs into coats."

Even Konrad got the idea and pretended he didn't need his coat, although actually the coat he was wearing was little more than a jacket, and a thin one at that. "It isn't," he said, "as if we were cowboys on the Great Plains and couldn't find any buffalo to make robes of while we counted our herds and added up our profits."

"No, no," the men of Linsk said and shook their heads. "Nothing like that."

"It is not as if we came from Finsk," Stefan said.

"Or Pinsk," Mikhail said.

"Or Zinsk," Tomasz said.

"Or Minsk," Konrad said. He was almost crying. And to tell the truth none of the others felt very happy.

"I've been thinking," Hilarion said. "Since I came, you businessmen have been too busy looking after me to have time to go to your houses to get proper coats."

Some of the men of Linsk nodded yes and some shook no. Then they thought about it and shook yes and nodded no.

"And the coats I've brought you clearly won't do for successful American businessmen."

The men of Linsk didn't know whether to shake or nod, so they sat very still and looked sick.

"So what I've decided," Hilarion said, "is that I should get you some coats from the used-clothing shop downstairs."

"But you have no money, Hilarion," Mikhail said.

"Oh, yes, I have," Hilarion said, and he showed them the gold coin the mayor had picked up in the street. In a minute he was gone, and in five minutes he was back, his arms full of coats. Then he had to tell them all about the talking box, which he had forgotten to mention before.

The men of Linsk were amazed by the story. They were amazed by the gold coin. They were amazed by the coats Hilarion brought them. But most of all they were amazed by the mayor's card.

"Now, Hilarion," Stefan said, "you have two things you must do tomorrow. First, you must visit the mayor, but then you must unfailingly go to the watchmaker's. Do you understand?"

"Three things," Hilarion said. "First of all I must give the shawl and the doll to Mr. Murphy."

"What a surprise," Konrad said. "There is always a man in the talking box. But I think that is more amazing than doing the trick the way they always pretend, with needles and springs and little grooves."

The men of Linsk all agreed, and they all lay down to sleep, wrapped in the warm coats Hilarion gave them. The coats were not new but they were thick and good, and the men of Linsk all dreamed that they were already prosperous and that their families were with them.

8.
When Is a Bear Not a Bear?

※※※※※※※※※

The next morning they finished the pie. They worried then about their supper, but they would have worried less if they had known that Hilarion still had the pocketful of pennies he had got from Redbeard and Blackbeard for lifting the wonderful talking box into the wagon. Hilarion didn't mention the pennies simply because he had forgotten them himself. However, the men of Linsk were hopeful. They believed now in Hilarion's luck and were sure that something would turn up, that perhaps the watchmaker would pay him his first day's pay out of hand. They should have known that Hilarion's luck didn't work that way.

They all put on their new coats and got ready to go out into the streets. They didn't even mind leaving the warm room, because they wanted to try out their coats against a really cold day.

"These are very American coats," Stefan said as he looked at himself and the others.

"Perhaps they will help us get work," Mikhail said.

"Perhaps people will see that men with such coats must be good workmen," Tomasz said.

"Perhaps people will think we are too rich to need work," Konrad said. And they all went out into the street laughing. Hilarion went with them with his great bearskin coat buttoned up to his chin and the shaggy head of the bear pulled down around his ears.

Hilarion found Mr. Murphy on his corner as usual, and Mr. Murphy understood at once what Hilarion wanted him to do with the shawl and the doll. He smiled at Hilarion, which was as good as a promise, and he held out his hand to Hilarion.

Hilarion had seen enough of Americans by now to know they shook hands a lot, so he shook Mr. Murphy's hand, being careful not to hurt him with the claws of his great bearskin mittens.

Hilarion then set out in a very businesslike way for the watchmaker's.

He was almost there, in fact, when he stopped at a corner to wait until a policeman should let him cross. There was a dense crowd of people around him, and he felt someone pressing up against him and taking his arm. He looked down and saw that it was a blind man.

"Would you please help me across the street?" the blind man said.

"Shall I help you across the street?" Hilarion said. So when the policeman told them to cross, they crossed the street together.

"Thank you very much," the blind man said, but he didn't let go of Hilarion's arm.

"Is there somewhere else you would like to go?" Hilarion said. And since the blind man now seemed to be tending off to the left, Hilarion went along with him, although that wasn't at all the way to the watchmaker's.

When at last they came to a quiet street, the blind man stopped, but still he didn't let go of Hilarion's arm.

"Is there anything else I can do for you now?" Hilarion said.

"Tell me," the blind man said, "are you a bear? You feel like a bear and you smell like a bear and you talk like a bear."

"Is there somewhere you would like to go?" Hilarion said.

"You are as strong as a bear, but you're rather large for a bear. Are you a white bear? I hear they are very large indeed. Are you white?"

"Is there someone you need to find?" Hilarion said. "I really should get to work, you know."

"You aren't an American bear, of that I'm sure," the blind man said. "And I'd say by the feel of your fur and the smell of your skin that you might come from Linsk, where the best bears are."

Hilarion heard the word Linsk and laughed with delight.

"Here, now," the blind man said, "I hope you aren't a bad-tempered, roaring bear." He felt Hilarion's hand.

"You've got claws enough. And teeth, too, I warrant, if only I could reach them."

"Please," Hilarion said, "just let me help you."

"Are you looking for work?" the blind man said suddenly. "My dancing bear has run away to join the circus, and without him I can't earn any money to support myself."

The blind man's voice was so sad that Hilarion said, "There must be something I can do."

Quick as a wink the blind man reached under his coat and brought out a chain and a collar. And all in a flash Hilarion became a dancing bear.

The blind man had a very large pocket in his coat, and out of this pocket he took a very small violin of the kind called a kit. Then he led Hilarion — or Hilarion led him — through streets and squares while he played and Hilarion danced.

"You're the best bear I ever had," the blind man said as they sat on a sunny bench in a small park, sharing the blind man's lunch. "And I have had black bears and brown bears, American bears and bears from the old country. I can't tell you all the bears I've had, but never before have the people clapped and shouted so and never have the coins rained into the cup in such numbers."

And that was no wonder, for Hilarion had been doing a great variety of country dances he had learned coming over on the ship. He did a squatting, kicking dance from Russia and a leaping, whirling dance from Turkey. He borrowed a handkerchief and did a Greek handkerchief dance. And he borrowed a sword and did a Serbian sword dance. He even borrowed a hat and did a Mexican hat dance, although no one has ever explained what a Mexican was doing on that ship going from Europe to America. In short, Hilarion was the most remarkable dancing bear that ever was.

Late in the afternoon, Hilarion was dancing on a busy corner in front of a bank. He hadn't been paying much attention to where they went in their wanderings, and in truth they had wandered back to that very corner were he had met the woman and the child and where he had talked with Mr. Murphy. He didn't recognize the place because he was now on the other side of the street and had approached from a different direction.

He was in the midst of a Spanish flamenco dance, sweating and stamping and clashing his teeth for castanets, when suddenly behind him there was a great shouting and whistle blowing and pistol shooting.

"Oh, my," said the blind man, "don't hurt my bear."

Hilarion turned just in time to see two men in masks run out of the bank. In their right hands they carried pistols and in their left hands they carried heavy canvas bags. They turned right only to see Mr. Murphy walking slowly along the street, speaking here and nodding there, and dipping into his pocket for some hot chestnuts he had bought at a brazier.

The robbers skidded to a stop and began to run in the other direction. Before they knew where they were, they had run smack into Hilarion, who simply wrapped his arms around them and held them off the ground. Their feet went right on kicking as if they didn't know yet that they weren't still running on the pavement. Their pistols flew out of their hands, and the heavy bags they carried dropped to the sidewalk and burst open. Gold flew everywhere. There was a carpet of gold around Hilarion's feet.

The people standing around began to dive for the gold, but just then Hilarion said sternly to the robbers, "Here now, what's the meaning of this?" Everyone thought that it was an angry bear growling, so no one dared move a step toward the gold.

Mr. Murphy came up then, finishing his chestnuts. He knew there was no hurry. Carefully he folded the paper bag and put it back in his pocket. Slowly he took his handcuffs out of another pocket and found the robbers' arms in Hilarion's fur. Gravely he attached the handcuffs to their wrists, and gently he said, "All right, Hilarion, you can set them down."

The robbers were glad to be set down and were very glad to be led off to a nice, safe jail where, no doubt, they would dream of claws and teeth and wake up delighted to be where they were.

Even before Hilarion set the robbers down, the manager came out of the bank with a dustpan and broom and began to sweep up the gold. When he had it all collected and poured into fresh bags, he took out a handful and filled the blind man's cup.

The blind man was an honest man of business and he immediately gave one of the coins to his bear as his day's wages. "And worth every penny of it," the blind man said, whether or not there was anyone there to understand him.

The crowd was there and they all nodded yes.

The bank manager was there and he nodded a most decided yes.

And Mr. Murphy was there, and he said, "Hilarion is indeed worth every penny of it. And more." He felt in his pocket and popped his last chestnut into Hilarion's mouth.

Hilarion knew that now the blind man had a cupful of gold he would be able to buy another bear, a very decent kind of bear to dance for him and to share his lunch. So Hilarion took off the collar and chain and gave them back to the blind man.

"You, too?" the blind man said. "Off to the circus, I suppose. It's the same with all you young fellows. The quiet life is too dull for you. I think that next time I'll advertise for a calm lady bear of settled habits and mature years. Perhaps she'll like this gentle, strolling life, a little music, a little dance, a sandwich in the park. What life could be better?"

Then Hilarion and the blind man said goodby with good feeling on both sides. They were both well pleased with their day's work.

As he was about to lead off the robbers, Mr. Murphy

said, "I found them, Hilarion. I gave the woman the shawl and I gave the child the doll."

"Did you find them today?" Hilarion said.

Mr. Murphy held out his empty hands, and Hilarion knew what he meant.

The bank manager looked carefully at Hilarion. "Why, I don't believe you are a bear at all," he said.

"Thank you very much for helping the blind man," Hilarion said.

"You don't talk like a bear any more than I do," the manager said.

"I've got to be going home now," Hilarion said.

"Come see me in the morning," the manager said. "I could use a man like you." But then he saw that Hilarion didn't understand a word he said, so he took out his notebook and drew a clock. He made the clock say nine o'clock.

Hilarion nodded.

The manager pointed into the bank and he pointed at the paper.

Hilarion nodded again.

The manager acted out sleeping, waking up, eating breakfast. Then he pointed into the bank and he pointed at the paper.

Hilarion nodded and smiled.

"I'll be here at nine o'clock tomorrow morning," Hilarion said. And he went home.

9.
Are We Still Friends?

On the way home, Hilarion bought a great roast of beef already cooked, and he bought a huge loaf of twisted bread, all brown and shiny, that made him think of home, and he bought another enormous pot of tea. He even bought a large bag of chestnuts, because he had been longing for chestnuts ever since Mr. Murphy had popped that single one into his mouth. He knew also that his friends would like chestnuts, that the taste of chestnuts would make then think of home.

Hilarion also stopped at the used-clothes store and bought four pairs of stout American boots. The boots were used, to be sure, but the soles were thick and the heels were true and the tops were strong. They would be warm and dry and make life much easier for his friends as they went about the city trying to find him a job. For, truly, Hilarion thought that when the men of Linsk spoke of finding work they meant finding work for him. He thought, in fact, that they were trying so hard to find him work that they were neglecting their own offices and wearing out their boots and were too busy to go home to get more. That was why he was so glad he had thought of boots for them.

"Hilarion got paid," the men of Linsk said when they saw him come in with his arms full of good things and boots.

Stefan and Mikhail allowed Konrad to inspect the boots while they set out the food, and Tomasz whistled and sang and sharpened his knives.

"Very good boots," Konrad said at last. He knew what the boots were and what they were not. They were not fancy or graceful. But they were plain boots made to be comfortable for much work or much walking. The men who had made them knew what they were about. Of course Konrad would have done some things differently, but still he knew good honest work when he saw it. "Very fine, Hilarion," he said. "You chose very fine boots."

By then the food was ready. Tomasz carved the roast. He was so pleased to be cutting meat again that he really would almost rather cut than eat. And that was a good thing, because the others ate so fast and so much that he was kept busy carving and had no time to eat until they were done. Then, when there was no one left to carve for but himself, he began to eat. He ate very slowly in order to be able to look forward to cutting the next slice, which he did with a flick of his wrist like a magician, and, presto, there was a broad, even slice on the plate.

Finally not even Tomasz could eat any more, although he continued to look at the roast with great affection. It was then that Mikhail said, "Hilarion, we have something to tell you."

"We've talked it all over," Stefan said.

"That's right," Tomasz said.

"To tell the truth — " Stefan said.

" — we've told a lie," Konrad said.

Hilarion looked at them in amazement. He didn't believe that in all his life anyone had ever told him a lie. To be sure, things were often not what they seemed. He had often heard of lies. But never before had he met one face to face.

"A lie?" Hilarion said.

"We ask you to forgive us," Konrad said.

"A real lie?" Hilarion said.

"We were ashamed to tell the truth," Stefan said.

"We are more ashamed now," Mikhail said.

"What kind of lie?" Hilarion asked. He didn't really want to know, but he couldn't think of anything else to say.

"We were ashamed to let you know that we — " Stefan began.

" — that we were so poor," Konrad said quickly. The men of Linsk had agreed to admit they were failures, but it was still very hard for them. To have come from Linsk with all that hope, all that skill, all that will to get on in the world, and to fail — it was almost more than they could face.

"Then you are not rich American businessmen?" Hilarion said.

"No," Stefan said.

"We were not even very American until you gave us these coats and these boots," Mikhail said. But they were all too sad then to think about the fine boots.

"I thought today," Tomasz said, "that I almost had a job. The man liked my coat — I could tell. And he liked my knives. And I like a man who knows good knives. But he didn't like my hat. It was very clear he didn't like my hat."

"Can you forgive us, Hilarion?" Konrad said.

"Oh, my friends," Hilarion said. He hugged them each, being very careful not to break their bones.

"Are we really still friends?" Konrad said.

"Hats," Hilarion shouted and ran downstairs.

He came back with his arms full of hats, the most American hats he could find. For Mikhail he had a red plaid cap with earflaps. "What the lumberjacks use in the north woods," he said. "Just the hat for a carpenter. People will think you have chosen and cut the trees yourself and brought them into town."

"I have done that, too," Mikhail said, "and would do it again if only I could find the forest."

For Stefan he had an enormous white cowboy's hat. "Just the thing for a tailor," he said. "It will look as if the light in your shop is so strong you have to shade your eyes while you take those wonderful tiny stitches."

For Konrad he had a fisherman's oilskin hat with a big brim in back. He put it on Konrad's head and said, "Now you look like a man with so much work in his shop that you don't have time to fix the roof and you wear the hat to keep the leaks from running down your neck."

"Oh, Hilarion," Konrad said, "you are so silly." But he was pleased with the hat and felt it all around and tried to see it in the broad, polished blade of Tomasz's cleaver.

And for Tomasz, Hilarion had a hard, flat straw hat. It was exactly the hat butchers wear summer and winter. He put it on Tomasz's head and cocked it on one side.

"Now you really are a butcher," Hilarion said. And that was all there was to say about that.

Now that the excitement of the roast and the bread was past, now that even the chestnuts had been eaten while no one was really looking, now that the lie had been confessed and forgiven, now that the hats were properly worn and admired, now they remembered the boots.

They put on the boots and at once they began to snap their fingers and dance. They moved slowly and stamped lightly, but as they warmed to it, the stove rattled and the windows shook. They jumped on the trunk and over it, and they danced so hard that the neighbors came up from downstairs and down from up-

stairs and across from over the alley and over from across the hall. They all danced and drank tea, and before it was time for bed, they all had beef sandwiches without worrying about whether there was enough for tomorrow — which there was.

As they were falling asleep, Stefan said happily, "And tomorrow we will all find work, and Hilarion will go again to the watchmaker's."

"But I didn't go to the watchmaker's," Hilarion said. And he had to tell them the whole marvelous adventure of the dancing bear.

10.

The Streetcar to Philadelphia

In the morning, the others were all up before Hilarion. Being a dancing bear was very hard work, and he was tired. They had a conference and knew just what they were going to do.

"Hilarion," Stefan said as they were making their breakfast of cold beef and tea warmed over on the stove. "Hilarion," he said, "today we are all going to go with you to the watchmaker's."

"Why, thank you very much," Hilarion said. "It will be good to have company on the way."

"It will be good to be with you, Hilarion," Konrad said, "but —

"Now, look here, Hilarion," Tomasz said. "You are a very good fellow and we all like you very much, but you must admit that two days ago you were supposed to go to the watchmaker's and you never got there."

"I never did," Hilarion said.

"And the day after that," Stefan said, "you were supposed to go to the watchmaker's and the mayor's — and what did you do?"

"Something came up," Hilarion said. He was beginning to feel that perhaps he hadn't done what he should have done.

"And today," Mikhail said, "you've got to go to the watchmaker's, the mayor's, and the bank manager's. But today we are all going to go with you to make sure you get to all those places."

"Oh, thank you, thank you," Hilarion said. "I'm always forgetting what I'm supposed to do, no matter how much I try to do the right thing."

"That's right, Hilarion," Konrad said. "You always try to do the right thing, and it always is the right thing, but somehow it's never at all what we expected."

Then they all put on their coats and boots. And Stefan put on his cowboy hat. And Mikhail put on his lumberjack hat. And Tomasz put on his butcher hat. And Konrad put on his fisherman hat. Of course, Hilarion put on his bearskin coat and hat and mittens and boots.

"First," Stefan said, "we'll go to the mayor's office, and to save time we'll take a streetcar."

They all went to the corner and exchanged smiles and handshakes with Mr. Murphy. Then they ran to catch their streetcar. It came toward them, rocking and roaring on the tracks. The trolley snapped and cracked against the overhead wire and showered sparks on the top of the car. When they climbed in, the car smelled of used electricity.

"It must be Hallowe'en," the motorman said. He

rolled his eyes at their hats, and everyone who understood English laughed. The rest of the people smiled even if they didn't know the joke. There was something about Hilarion that made people happy when they looked at him.

Hilarion held out a pawful of coins.

"Five?" the motorman said.

"For all of us," Hilarion said.

Of course they didn't understand each other, but the motorman had driven streetcars for a long time and knew what to do. He held up his hand with all his fingers spread. "Five?" he said.

"Five," Hilarion said. He held up five claws.

The motorman picked out enough coins for five fares and dropped them into the box. The box began to whir and click, and Hilarion thought it was grinding the coins up — perhaps into straw.

When they had lurched and stumbled to their seats in the rocketing car and could look around them, Hilarion said, "Look, there's the woman with the shawl."

Sure enough. There she was with the shawl around her. And the child and the doll were standing up in the seat, looking back at them over the woman's shoulder.

Hilarion was just about to get up and go to her when the car stopped with a jerk that threw him forward and then back into his seat. The doors opened and two men got in. At least they were probably men, although one wore a chalk-white skeleton mask, and the other wore the pale porcelain mask of a Chinese woman, with slanting eyes, smudgy floating-cloud eyebrows, and scarlet lips.

"Don't anybody move," the Chinese woman said. The voice was clearly a man's voice, very deep and harsh, very scary coming out of that delicate face.

"We're taking this car to Philadelphia," the skeleton said.

"You're crazy," the motorman said.

"Shut up, you," the Chinese woman said. And both men showed pistols and waved them about. The car was very quiet.

"Start it up," the skeleton said. "Let's go." He began turning the crank to change the sign from CITY HALL.

"There's no PHILADELPHIA on there," the motorman said. "This is a city car."

"We'll put up the SPECIAL sign," the skeleton said. "No, here's NOT IN SERVICE. That will do as well."

"Get started," the Chinese woman said. He laid his pistol against the motorman's ear. "Don't stop for anybody."

"But I can't go to Philadelphia," the motorman said.

"Just get started," the skeleton said, "and we'll get to Philadelphia."

"Anybody knows," the Chinese woman said, "that streetcar lines connect all over the country. I could have said, 'Take us to Washington.' Or, 'Take us to Boston.' Or even, 'Take us to Cleveland.' But I want to go to Philadelphia, and we'd better get started."

"And while my friend entertains the driver," the skeleton said, "I will pass among you and take up a collection."

He began to go from seat to seat and collect from the men watches and rings and stickpins and cufflinks and from the women watches and rings and necklaces and brooches and bracelets. And from all of them he collected all the money they had.

From the men of Linsk he collected nothing, because they had nothing to give him. He stood beside Hilarion in disgust and took a box from under his arm and placed it on Hilarion's lap. "Here," he said, "hold this." Of course Hilarion didn't know what he said, but he clutched the box to keep it from sliding off his slippery bearskin lap.

"Pay attention here," the skeleton said to everyone in the car. "This friendly bear is now holding a box on his lap, and that box is a bomb that can go off any time you don't all do exactly as I say."

"But you'll be blown up, too," the motorman said.

"That doesn't matter," the skeleton said. "I have to go to Philadelphia."

"We'll have to turn the car around," the motorman said.

"So we'll turn the car around," the Chinese woman said. "But no tricks or you'll join my skeleton friend in the graveyard tonight."

The motorman stopped the car, and he and the

Chinese woman got out and walked to the back of the car. They unhooked the control rope and pulled the trolley away from the wire and walked back around the car, holding the rope so that the trolley reversed and pointed back the other way, and the back of the car became the front. They carefully let the trolley spring back against the wire and they anchored the rope. Then they took a heavy iron bar and switched the tracks so the car could go the other way.

Meanwhile, the skeleton went on with his collection. When he came to the woman with the shawl, he snatched the shawl from her shoulders and said, "Just what I need to carry this stuff."

Of course Hilarion would have been very angry if he had seen this, but Hilarion just then was much more interested in the box he was holding. It was a ticking box, and ticking meant clocks, as he very well knew. Without stopping to remember the rules about opening other people's boxes, he reached into his pocket and brought out his watchmaker's eyeglass and his watchmaker's tiny screwdriver and his watchmaker's fine tweezers for holding fine parts.

Soon he had the box opened, and he looked inside. Indeed, there was a clock in there. It was a very poor sort of clock and would have had hard work ticking at any time, but poor as it was he felt sorry for it, all packed and jammed and tied up in the crowded box. Hilarion believed in fair play for any clock, no matter how poor.

The motorman climbed back into the car, and the Chinese woman prepared to follow him. "And now for Philadelphia," the Chinese woman said as he took one last look around before mounting the steps.

At that moment, Hilarion handed the box back to the skeleton. "I fixed your box," he said.

The skeleton made a gesture of impatience and then he screamed. "It's stopped ticking. It's going to explode." And he dove out the door, and he and the Chinese woman ran away as fast as they could go.

For a moment everyone in the car was frightened, but Hilarion held up three sticks of dynamite taped together. "I don't know how they expected the clock to run with all this dirt in the works," Hilarion said.

"You'd better let me have that," the motorman said, and he took the dynamite and put it in his pocket. "I'll just hand this to Mr. Murphy when we pass his corner. He'll know what to do with it."

The passengers laughed and clapped and cheered Hilarion, and they were happy as they sorted through the skeleton's collection for their things.

"Well," a man said, "I see that you are not only strong but clever. You have saved us from being robbed and blown up and taken to Philadelphia. How can we ever thank you properly?"

Hilarion looked then and saw it was the very same man who had been in the talking box. Hilarion recognized the fine suit and the magnificent overcoat, fur-lined and with a rich fur collar. He recognized the fine shoes and the fine gloves. And he particularly recognized the fine diamond stickpin, which he appreciated all the more now that he had his watchmaker's glass in his eye. Anyone, of course, could recognize the gold watch the man now put in his pocket and the gold chain fit to anchor a steamer.

"Good morning, Mr. Mayor," they all said.

11.
Happily Ever After

The motorman got out and switched the switch and changed the trolley again so they could all go where they wanted to go and not to Philadelphia. The mayor made a speech about the things Hilarion had done to save them all in the streetcar and to save him in the talking box. He even had Mr. Murphy's report about the time Hilarion saved the child under the wagon. He took the notebook out of his pocket and showed Hilarion's name and the star.

The mayor hadn't yet heard about how Hilarion caught the bank robbers, but the bank manager stood up and told all about it. He was on his way to see his mother and just happened to be on that car.

As for the mayor, he often rode the cars in order to see the people of his city and learn what they talked about and what they wanted and what they didn't like. This morning he was riding back from an early and very unsatisfactory interview with the men who were building his new house up in the wild regions about the Central

Park. The work was not going at all to his liking. The men simply didn't seem to know their business.

"I'd like to send you up there to knock their heads together," he said to Hilarion.

Hilarion looked puzzled. He knew the mayor was angry, but he didn't know what was making him angry.

"What is he saying?" he said to the men of Linsk, but of course they couldn't tell him.

"Why is he angry?" he said to the woman with the shawl. But she knew no more about it than he did.

However, the child was going to school, and she knew English perfectly. She was able to tell Hilarion what the mayor said, and she was able to tell the mayor what Hilarion said. So the mayor and Hilarion sat down on the seat, and the child and the doll stood between them.

"I don't suppose you would care to go and build my house," the mayor said. "And thank you for the doll." This last wasn't really something the mayor said, but it was something the child added on her own when she was telling Hilarion what the mayor said. She knew it wasn't polite to break into other people's conversations, but she just had to tell him how much she loved the doll.

"It was Mikhail who made it," Hilarion said. "But I'm not a carpenter," he said to the mayor.

"More's the pity," the mayor said.

Hilarion was shy about talking with the mayor, but the child was so pleased with the doll that she had end-less faith in the craft of the man who made it. So the next thing Hilarion seemed to say was, "I am a very good

82

fellow, and I have a friend who is an even better fellow and who is a carpenter." The mayor looked queerly at Hilarion.

"And where is this fine fellow?" the mayor said.

"Right here," Hilarion said, "and, oh, he made my wonderful doll." The mayor now began to understand what was happening, and he thought none the worse of Hilarion for having good and loyal friends.

The men of Linsk were all gathered around the mayor and Hilarion and the child. They had turned a seat around so that the woman could sit facing her child, and Mikhail sat with her. Stefan and Tomasz kneeled on the seat behind her, and Konrad kneeled behind the child on another seat. Other people gathered to hear.

"So you're a carpenter?" the mayor said.

"Of course I'm a carpenter," Mikhail said. "I'm the most wonderful carpenter who ever lived. Just look at this marvelous doll. Just look at it." The mayor could scarcely avoid looking at it, for it was very close to battering his nose.

"But can you build a house?" the mayor said.

"I can build anything," Mikhail said. "Houses, palaces, city halls, pyramids, steamships. And I can do it better than anyone in the whole world. I'll need to see the plans first."

The mayor, fortunately, was able to discover in all of this exactly what Mikhail had actually said in the short, modest speech he had actually made. "Good," the mayor said. He looked at his watch. "Come to my office at four o'clock. Bring the child so we can talk. We'll go look at the house and the plans and see where we are. And I am certainly the luckiest mayor in the world to find a man who can make such dolls."

Mikhail looked strangely at the mayor, but the mayor knew the child must have added something on her own.

"Hurrah," Konrad shouted. "Mikhail has a job."

"And who is that?" the mayor said, turning to look at Konrad. "Some fisherman, I suppose."

"I am Konrad," Konrad said, "and I am a most wonderful man. Such a shoemaker you never saw. I can make shoes for kings and emperors and mayors. I can make boots for a whole army or glass slippers for the finest lady who ever lived. I can spin straw into gold if only I have a chance."

Once again the mayor marveled at a language in which Konrad could say two words that meant so much.

"You mustn't mind my child," the woman said. "She tells such stories." But only Hilarion and the men of Linsk understood her, for her remark never found its way into English.

"I suppose this is your child," the mayor said.

"Oh, yes," the woman said. "I am her mother and I am the most wonderful mother in the whole world. I work hard all day and am tired out at night, and I tell the most wonderful stories about princes and princesses and enchantments and spells. See my wonderful shawl." The child spread the end of the shawl for the mayor to see.

84

"Wonderful," the mayor said.

"Wonderful," the bank manager said as he bent to examine it.

"You can't even see where it was torn," the woman said. "Stefan the tailor mended it. He could mend the emperor's new clothes with magic thread."

"I wish I needed a tailor," the bank manager said. He shook his head. "You don't often see work like that. But the truth is that what I need is a butcher."

It happened that the bank looked after some property for an old lady who couldn't look after it herself. Part of the property was a butcher shop that wasn't doing as well as it should.

"What I need," the bank manager said, "is a good butcher who is honest and who can talk with people from Linsk. It's a whole neighborhood of people from Linsk."

Tomasz spoke up. "I am a butcher," he said. "And I am surely not from Zinsk." It sounded to the bank manager, however, exactly as if he had said, "I am the most wonderful butcher in the whole world. I can slice meat so thin you can see through it, so tender it melts in your mouth. I can truss a roast or dress a fowl to your heart's desire. My knives are so sharp you can shave with them or slice up milkweed floating in the air."

"Oh, that's too bad," the bank manager said. He had caught the word Zinsk in what Tomasz had said. "The people there hate anyone from Zinsk."

"But he is from Linsk," Konrad said. "We are all

really from Linsk, although we haven't liked to admit it."

"Why should you be ashamed to admit it?" the mayor said.

"We weren't ashamed to admit it," Konrad said. "We were afraid Linsk would be ashamed of us for being such failures."

"Well," the mayor said, "I don't think anyone is a failure who has such friends as you all have in each other, who sticks to his friends and rejoices in their good fortune, and particularly anyone who has such a friend as Hilarion."

Before the child told the others what the mayor had said, she kissed him heartily and let him kiss the doll.

"Aha," the bank manager said, "since you are really from Linsk, just come to the bank at three o'clock, and we'll go to the butcher shop and make our arrangements, although I must say that your clothes won't look quite right to the people from Linsk."

"My trunk is full of clothes for them," Hilarion said.

"And some decent hats, I hope," the mayor said.

The men of Linsk all looked at one another's hats and burst out laughing.

"Good hats from Linsk," Hilarion said.

"Just what is needed," the mayor said. "The hats they are wearing don't look very serious somehow."

"Hurrah," Konrad said. "Mikhail and Tomasz have jobs."

"He's a very generous fellow," the mayor said, "for someone who doesn't have a job himself. I like that."

"Nor do I, Stefan, the wonderful tailor, have a job either." Stefan said all this in a very small cough.

"Oh, as to Stefan," the woman said. "The owner of the shop where I work saw the mending of my shawl and wants to meet the tailor who did it. We need a master workman at our place."

"Hurrah," Konrad said, "Mikhail and Tomasz and Stefan have jobs. But what about me? What about good, kind, and generous Konrad?"

"Silly," the child said, "old Jan, who has the shoe shop on the ground floor of our very own house, is looking for someone to work with him and take the business over some day, and besides I want Konrad to be very near."

"Hurrah," Hilarion said, "Mikhail and Tomasz and Stefan and Konrad all have jobs, and Linsk will be proud of them."

"Now we can send for our wives and children," the men of Linsk said.

"But what about Hilarion?" the mayor said.

Just then the blind man pushed his way through the crowd. "It's my bear," he cried. "I'd know his voice anywhere." He threw his arms around Hilarion. "Oh, bear," he said, "you didn't run away to join the circus. You were coming back to dance for me, weren't you?"

Unfortunately, whatever language the blind man spoke, it wasn't one that anyone in the car understood, so no one knew what he was saying. He shyly offered Hilarion the chain and collar, but Hilarion gently put it aside.

"Oh, do come," the blind man said. "I've already found another bear. There would be two of you. You'd be such company for each other. She's very dear. A steady, sober sort of person. Very warm and kind. You'd like her."

But finally the blind man understood that Hilarion wouldn't go with him, and he went back to his seat.

"Yes," the men of Linsk said, "what about Hilarion?"

"I have my job at the watchmaker's," Hilarion said.

"For now," the mayor said. "Then we'll see."

"Yes," the bank manager said. "We'll see."

"But where will he live?" the men of Linsk said.

Hilarion opened his mouth to say he'd get along somehow, but out came, "Oh, I am such a wonderful fellow that I'll have to go and stay with the woman and the child. After all, the child has no one to play with, and the woman has no one to talk to after I — I mean the child — am — I mean is — in bed."

Then they all laughed and were pleased with themselves and each other.